JOY IN SORROW, HOPE FOR TOMORROW

Reunion

JOY IN SORROW, HOPE FOR TOMORROW

Reunion

VONNETTA MAYO

gatekeeper press
Tampa, Florida

This book is a work of fiction. The names, characters and events in this book are the products of the author's imagination or are used fictitiously. Any similarity to real persons living or dead is coincidental and not intended by the author.

The content associated with this book is the sole work and responsibility of the author. Gatekeeper Press had no involvement in the generation of this content.

Joy in Sorrow, Hope for Tomorrow:
Reunion

Published by Gatekeeper Press
7853 Gunn Hwy., Suite 209
Tampa, FL 33626
www.GatekeeperPress.com

Copyright © 2025 by Vonnetta Mayo

All rights reserved. Neither this book, nor any parts within it may be sold or reproduced in any form or by any electronic or mechanical means, including information storage and retrieval systems, without permission in writing from the author. The only exception is by a reviewer, who may quote short excerpts in a review.

Library of Congress Control Number: 2024947645

ISBN (hardcover): 9781662958151
ISBN (paperback): 9781662958168
eISBN: 9781662958175

DEDICATION

This book is dedicated to my late grandmother,
Demmie Dell Goodlow. May you always be remembered.
Rest in heaven, Grandma.
Love always!

Vonnetta

While you read this book, I pray that God
opens your mind, gives you understanding and clarity,
so that you can enjoy this book in its entirety.
I know this book will exhilarate your spirit.
Joy in Sorrow, Hope for Tomorrow: Reunion is
an inspiring book everyone can enjoy.

CHAPTER 1

The Journey

We were walking with one purpose in mind: freedom. My mother, Ana Mae; my three brothers, Billy, Elmer, and John; and I, Betsy, were all focused on reaching our destination in North Carolina. All I could think about was my father. I thought about how he looked and what he would do when he saw us.

As we continued, unsure of how far we still had to go, my mother turned to us and said, "Tell me when you need to rest. We are free now! We are no longer on anyone's time."

"Yes, ma'am. We will," we replied.

John asked, "Will we eat tonight?"

"Of course. God will provide," my mother answered. Her calmness reassured me; not a trace of worry crossed her face.

She began singing a spiritual hymn, and soon we joined her, our voices rising with the memory of the songs she and her friends once sang in the shed. Lost in the joy of singing, we didn't even notice how far we had walked.

My mother smiled as she looked back at us and said, "Let's rest now." We sat under the shade of a tree, its coolness a welcome relief.

Billy spoke, "Are we walking all the way to North Carolina?"

"No," my mother replied. "We'll catch a ride in a carriage when there's room."

My brothers and I exchanged smiles, relieved that soon we'd be off our feet.

After resting, my mother stood up. "Stay here," she instructed us. "I'll see what I can find for us to eat."

John cheered, "Yes!"

We watched her walk toward the carriages.

"I can't wait to get to North Carolina," Elmer said.

"Me either," I added.

As evening fell, my brothers grew drowsy, their heads nodding in exhaustion. I glanced toward the carriages, but my mother was nowhere in sight. As I bit my nails, I wondered, *Is everything all right*?

Before long, she returned with some food.

"I had to ask around a few carriages, but here it is," she said. It wasn't much, but we were grateful. "I told you, God would provide," she added.

We ate first, and she ate what was left.

Afterward, my mother told us, "The women and children are sleeping in the carriages tonight. Let's get ready."

As we walked toward the carriages, I wondered, *Will we still say "Our Nightly Prayer" now that we're free?*

When we arrived, my mother helped us climb inside. A few women were already there, lying under thin white sheets, like the ones we used in the shed. My mother found two more sheets in the corner. She gave one to us, keeping the other for herself.

As we settled in, John asked, "Are we saying 'Our Nightly Prayer' tonight?"

"Of course," my mother replied. "Even when we're delivered, we must keep praying. Now, let's get ready to pray."

She began to teach us our new prayer.

We all begin to whisper,

"Oh, Lord, Father in heaven,
We thank you for our freedom.
You have freed us from being slaves.
You have taken us away from our evil master.

We worship and adore you.
We knew that you were the only one
Who could free us.
So we didn't complain and fuss
Because we knew one day, we were going to see you.

So we kept waiting,
Until that victorious and glorious day came.
We didn't sneak away from slavery and run.
We just kept praying.

While we were believing and trusting in you,
We still had joy in sorrow.
And that gave us hope for tomorrow
Because we knew soon came our breakthrough.
Lord, we love you. Amen."

My brothers and I curled up beneath the thin white sheet, and my mother did the same. She reminded us why we had to whisper "Our Nightly Prayer," so we wouldn't disturb the other women in the carriage.

"I'm glad we're here and not in that shed," Billy whispered.

"Me too," I agreed.

My mother smiled softly at us.

CHAPTER 2

The Provider

The next morning, we woke to an unfamiliar silence—no one shouting, "Get up and get to work!" It felt incredible to sleep and wake on our terms. Shortly after we awakened, the carriage came to a stop.

"I'm going to find us something to eat," my mother said.

"Yes, ma'am," we replied in unison, waiting patiently for her return. This time I had no doubt she'd come back with food.

When she did, my brothers and I ate first, as always, and then she finished what was left. There was a little more than last night, and I couldn't help but marvel at how things always seemed to turn out better than we expected.

After we ate, the women in the carriage began talking about how far we might be from the plantation.

"I wonder where we are now," my mother mused. "When I was searching for food, I heard someone say they think we're heading east, toward the Carolinas."

She smiled, and I couldn't contain myself.

I asked, "That's where Father is, right?"

Billy looked at me with concern, but my mother nodded.

"Yes," she confirmed, and my brothers and I smiled at the thought.

As the carriage began moving again, my mother said, "Next stop, we need to find somewhere to use the bathroom and get cleaned up. We've been in these dirty clothes for days."

"Yes, ma'am," we all replied.

There wasn't much to do in the carriage, so we got creative and came up with games. One of our favorites was "I Spy." We took turns saying, "I spy with my little eye," and then gave a letter for the object we were secretly looking at.

When it was my turn, I shouted, "I spy with my little eye something that starts with the letter F!"

John jumped in first. "Fence!"

I laughed. "No."

Next, Elmer guessed, "Frog," but he was wrong too.

Finally, Billy said, "I know—fly!"

I sighed. "That's it."

Now it was Billy's turn. He grinned and declared, "I spy with my little eye something that begins with the letter T!"

Without hesitation, I blurted, "Tree."

Billy shook his head, and I was stunned—I was sure I had it right.

Elmer took a shot. "Trash can."

"Nope," Billy said.

Then John, hesitantly, whispered, "Teeth."

We all burst into laughter.

"Wrong!" yelled Billy, and Elmer, spotting something in the distance, guessed, "Tent."

"Yep, that's it!" Billy exclaimed.

"I finally saw the tent in the back of the woods," Elmer added with a grin.

We kept playing "I Spy," having fun while challenging each other. But eventually, John stopped playing, unable to keep up. Occasionally, during the game, I'd glance over at my mother. She seemed deep in thought. I wouldn't say anything, but I would silently pray for her.

I wondered, *Is she thinking about Father?*

As the night wore on, we couldn't stop laughing, debating who had the most correct guesses in the game.

"I'm the oldest, so I should be the winner automatically," I teased.

Billy and Elmer exchanged glances and shouted, "No way!"

And we all erupted in laughter again. By then the carriage had come to a stop.

"I have to use the bathroom," John said, fidgeting.

Mother looked at him. "I'll take you," she said, getting up.

They stepped out of the carriage and headed into the woods. I heard her urge him to hurry because the carriage would be leaving soon. But before they knew it, the carriage started to pull away.

Frantically, my mother ran after it, waving her hands and shouting, "Stop! Stop!"

Finally, the driver halted, and she and John scrambled back inside, both breathing hard.

Wow, that was a close call, I thought. I don't know what I would've done if they'd been left behind.

One of the women in the carriage turned to my mother. "Are you all right?" she asked with concern.

Still catching her breath, Mother nodded. "Yes, I'm just glad the driver stopped in time."

Then, turning to us, she said, "Let's get ready to lie down."

We grabbed our thin white sheets and curled up underneath them.

Then we all begin to whisper,

"Oh, Lord, Father in heaven,
We thank you for our freedom.
You have freed us from being slaves.
You have taken us away from our evil master.

We worship and adore you.
We knew that you were the only one
Who could free us.
So we didn't complain and fuss
Because we knew one day, we were going to see you.

So we kept waiting,
Until that victorious and glorious day came.
We didn't sneak away from slavery and run.
We just kept praying.

While we were believing and trusting in you,
We still had joy in sorrow.
And that gave us hope for tomorrow
Because we knew soon came our breakthrough.
Lord, we love you. Amen."

While we were whispering, I noticed that the other women in the carriage were quietly watching us.

I couldn't help but think, *Maybe "Our Nightly Prayer" is starting to rub off on them. Maybe next time, they'll join us in saying it.*

CHAPTER 3

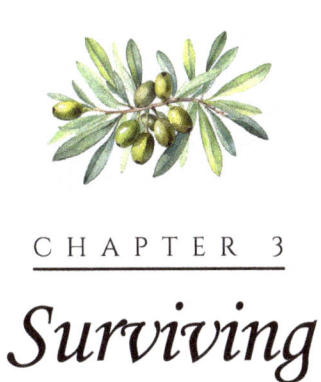

Surviving

When I woke up, my mother and the other women in the carriage were already awake, but my brothers were still fast asleep. I figured they were taking advantage of being able to sleep in for once. I, on the other hand, felt well rested and curious about where we were headed next. It almost felt like an adventure, not knowing where we were headed.

When my brothers *finally* woke up, my mother mentioned that she hoped the carriage would stop soon so she could find us something to eat.

She added, "Hopefully, there's a place to get cleaned up and use the bathroom."

The other women in the carriage nodded in agreement. Shortly after, the carriage slowed to a stop.

"Stay seated. I'll be right back," Mother instructed.

I noticed this stop looked different from the others. Instead of being surrounded by woods, there were houses everywhere.

"There sure are a lot of homes around here," I said.

"Yes, there are!" Billy and Elmer echoed, while John grinned, taking in the new surroundings.

A short while later, Mother returned with food. She told us a former slave had mentioned we were in Knoxville, Tennessee.

John asked eagerly, "What does that mean? Are we home yet?"

Mother shook her head. "No, we will not be home until we reach North Carolina. But this means there should be a place nearby where we can get cleaned up and use the bathroom."

The women in the carriage smiled at this news, and Mother added, "Now eat up so we can get off this carriage."

My brothers and I quickly dug into our food, and while we ate, I couldn't help but wonder how much farther we had to travel to North Carolina. I was growing anxious to see my father.

Once we finished eating, Mother helped us climb down from the carriage, with the other women following close behind. The warm, pleasant weather and bustling homes of Knoxville filled me with excitement. I hoped North Carolina would be just as nice.

Suddenly, John took off running.

Without hesitation, Mother sprinted after him, calling, "John, stop!" When he did, she caught her breath and scolded, "Don't you run off like that again, especially when I don't know where you're going!"

"Yes, ma'am," John mumbled, looking embarrassed.

The rest of us exchanged surprised glances—John usually only ran around with us, never away from Mother. But I figured he was just happy to stretch his legs after so much time in the carriage.

After that little scare, we made our way to a huge building with a long line of former slaves waiting to get inside.

Mother joined the line, and I asked, "Is this where we'll get cleaned up and use the bathroom?"

Mother nodded. "Yes, I believe so," she replied.

John interjected, "Good, because I really need to go!"

Elmer chuckled and teased, "You always do!"

John just gave him a look.

As we waited, I noticed the line growing longer behind us, and I was relieved we had arrived early. I hadn't realized just how many former slaves were traveling with us in the carriages. I tried to catch a glimpse of the local people through the crowd but couldn't see past the line. Meanwhile, John grew restless, shifting from foot to foot. I could tell he was getting desperate, and I hoped we'd get inside before he had an accident. Luckily, there were only a few people ahead of us.

When we entered the building, I was amazed at its size—it seemed even bigger on the inside. Mother quickly found the nearest restroom for John.

As he went in, I thought, *This has to be better than the outhouse.*

It was our first time using an indoor bathroom.

Once John finished, we made our way to a large room filled with other former slaves. Women were walking around, distributing clothes, towels, and soap. Mother received enough for my brothers and me but not for herself.

She handed the clothes to us and said, "Let me find out where we can change. Stay here, I'll be right back."

"Yes, ma'am," we answered.

As Mother disappeared into the crowd, Billy mused, "I wonder how far she has to go to find that out."

None of us responded, instead staring off into the busy room. I spotted the women from our carriage making their way over.

One of them asked, "Are you all alright? Is your mother nearby?"

"Yes, we're fine. She'll be back soon," I replied.

Elmer added, "She went to find out where we can change clothes."

The woman nodded and said, "Good. Everyone's taking turns in the restrooms, so your mother will return momentarily."

We grinned as they walked away.

Shortly after, Mother returned and confirmed, "We'll be using the restrooms to get changed."

John laughed and said, "That's what the other women told us!"

Mother smiled and led us to the restrooms.

There were plenty of restrooms, so we didn't have to wait long. Mother gave my brothers the soap and towels, and they went in first. While we waited, I noticed some of the former slaves holding small boxes.

"What's in those boxes?" I asked.

"I'm not sure," Mother replied.

"Maybe it's food," I guessed.

Mother remained silent.

When my brothers came out, it was our turn. I was mesmerized by the clean, bright restroom—so different from the outhouses we were used to.

"Start washing up," Mother urged, snapping me out of my daze.

Once we were clean and dressed, we followed Mother to a room where tables were stacked with boxes.

She opened one and exclaimed, "It is food!"

I grinned as she handed each of us a box. This was the first time we'd had two meals in one day. With no chairs, we sat on the floor in a corner and devoured our meals, a full meal—a sandwich, chips, and a drink. It felt good to see Mother eat her own food instead of our leftovers. This time there were no leftovers. My brothers and I ate everything quickly.

Afterward, Mother said, "It's been a long day. Let's find out if we'll be staying in the carriages tonight."

We left the room and found one of the women who had handed out the clothes.

"Will everyone be returning to the carriages tonight?" Mother asked.

The woman replied, "No, we've arranged for you all to stay in the old slave quarters for the night."

"Slave quarters?" Mother asked, surprised.

"Yes, but they've been transformed. Come, follow us."

As we walked, I wondered, *Are the slave quarters like the sheds we lived in on the plantation?*

Billy asked, "How far are they?"

No one answered; we just kept walking. It felt like it took forever. But when we finally arrived, the quarters were nothing like the sheds we were used to.

With a grin, the woman said, "This is where you'll be staying tonight."

Mother whispered, "Wow."

CHAPTER 4

Home Away from Home

When we stepped into the former slave quarter, it felt like a real home. There were actual beds and places to sit other than the floor—I was impressed! My brothers wasted no time, immediately jumping into the bottom bunk.

"Get out of that bed!" Mother scolded. "We haven't decided who's sleeping where yet."

With eight beds in total and eight of us staying there, Mother quickly decided, "My children will sleep in the four beds across from the window, and the rest of us can take the ones next to the window."

The other former slaves nodded in agreement. I could tell everyone was just thrilled to sleep in a real bed, so any spot would've been fine.

Finally, Mother announced, "Let's get ready to lie down!"

By now my brothers and I didn't need to ask if we were going to say "Our Nightly Prayer." We knew that no matter where we were, we would always end the day with prayer.

So, louder than usual, we begin to pray,

VONNETTA MAYO

"Oh, Lord, Father in heaven,
We thank you for our freedom.
You have freed us from being slaves.
You have taken us away from our evil master.

We worship and adore you.
We knew that you were the only one
Who could free us.
So we didn't complain and fuss
Because we knew one day, we were going to see you.

So we kept waiting,
Until that victorious and glorious day came.
We didn't sneak away from slavery and run.
We just kept praying.

While we were believing and trusting in you,
We still had joy in sorrow.
And that gave us hope for tomorrow
Because we knew soon came our breakthrough.
Lord, we love you. Amen."

When my brothers and I woke up the next morning, the other former slaves were gone, and Mother was still sound asleep in her bunk. Before my brothers could start horseplaying, I warned them not to make too much noise and wake her up. They agreed, but of course, they instantly started wrestling with each other.

JOY IN SORROW, HOPE FOR TOMORROW: REUNION

As I gazed out the window, I couldn't help but wonder where the others had gone. I felt a bit uneasy, but seeing Mother still asleep made me realize she must have been truly exhausted. I had never seen her sleep this long before.

Eventually, I couldn't resist joining in with my brothers, and we came up with different games to pass the time. We were having so much fun until John suddenly announced he needed to use the bathroom. That's when I realized, there wasn't a bathroom in the former slave quarter. Billy suggested we wake Mother up, and though I hesitated initially, I agreed.

I gently nudged Mother awake. She opened her eyes with a peaceful smile, making me feel guilty for disturbing her.

"John needs to use the bathroom," I explained.

"Okay," she replied softly. "How long have I been asleep?"

"A long time!" Elmer chimed in.

Mother chuckled, then got up and took John outside to the outhouse.

As they were leaving, Mother mentioned that once they returned, she'd go find us something to eat. That brightened my brothers' moods, and we waited patiently for them to come back. I sat on the bottom bunk while Billy and Elmer sprawled out on the floor, too tired to bother climbing back up to their top bunks.

When Mother and John finally returned, she explained that the delay was because there had been a long line for the outhouse.

John eagerly confirmed, "It really was!"

Mother also mentioned that while they were in line, she found out everyone else had gone back to the carriages to eat. She told us to prepare because we were heading back to the carriages ourselves.

Once there, Mother helped us climb in and said, "I'll be right back with some food."

As we settled in, I noticed the other women from the carriage sitting nearby eating sandwiches. They waved at us, and we waved back.

Suddenly, Elmer blurted, "I'm hungry!"

I reassured him, "Mother will be back shortly," and Billy nodded in agreement.

Not long after, Mother arrived with sandwiches and chips. Elmer's mood lifted immediately after eating, and we all felt a little better. "The carriage will be leaving soon," Mother informed us.

John then said, "I'm going to miss sleeping in those beds, they were so comfortable."

"I know," Mother replied. "Hopefully, our next stop has beds too."

As I sat there, I thought to myself, *I hope our next stop is home.*

The endless traveling was starting to wear on me, and I longed to finally be with Father.

CHAPTER 5

On the Road Again!

As the carriage pulled off, the other women began to curl up beneath their thin, white sheets, clearly worn out from the long day. I knew my mother had slept through much of the afternoon, but even so, she said, "Let's get ready to lie down."

We followed her lead, wrapping ourselves in our own thin, white sheets.

I doubted she could still be tired, but then she softly said, "Let us pray."

To my surprise, I noticed the other women quietly putting their hands together in prayer as well. It was a shared moment that brought a sense of peace to all of us.

When we all begin to whisper,

"Oh, Lord, Father in heaven,
We thank you for our freedom.
You have freed us from being slaves.
You have taken us away from our evil master.

VONNETTA MAYO

We worship and adore you.
We knew that you were the only one
Who could free us.
So we didn't complain and fuss
Because we knew one day, we were going to see you.

So we kept waiting,
Until that victorious and glorious day came.
We didn't sneak away from slavery and run.
We just kept praying.

While we were believing and trusting in you,
We still had joy in sorrow.
And that gave us hope for tomorrow
Because we knew soon came our breakthrough.
Lord, we love you. Amen."

After the prayer, I was amazed at how quickly the other women in the carriage had picked up on "Our Nightly Prayer." I guess they'd been listening to us all along.

Mother always said, "You never know who's watching and being encouraged by what you do." Now I truly understood her words.

The next morning, when I woke up, I overheard my mother and the other women talking about where we might be heading next.

Curious, I asked, "How far are we from North Carolina?"

My mother sighed and replied, "I'm not sure, but I hope we're still heading that way."

"Me too," I said gently.

Meanwhile, my brothers were already up and full of energy, playing as usual.

I watched them and thought, *These boys never run out of steam.*

But I didn't feel like joining in this time. All I wanted was to lie around and wait until we reached our next stop, hoping it would finally be the end of our journey. The sun felt hotter than usual, and I was thankful someone had placed a bucket of water in the carriage. It was as if they knew the heat would be relentless wherever we were going.

Eventually, I drifted back to sleep, only to be awakened by my mother's gentle voice.

"Are you okay?" she asked.

"Yes, ma'am, just tired," I replied.

She nodded and said, "This sun will drain you."

Seeing the worried expressions on my brothers' faces, I got up and took a long drink of water from the bucket.

"This should do the trick," I said with a grin.

My mother smiled, encouraged. Feeling a little more energized, I joined my brothers in their games. John, always enthusiastic, suggested we play "I Spy."

"Not again," groaned Billy and Elmer in unison.

"I like that game," John insisted.

"Me too," I confessed.

Reluctantly, Billy and Elmer agreed, and John beamed with excitement, declaring, "I'm going first!"

As we played, Billy and Elmer were more focused on teasing each other than on the game itself, while John was thrilled to be winning. Every time he guessed correctly, he would boast and shout in triumph, something that didn't happen often. I was happy for him.

When the game ended, John ran up to Mother, proudly announcing, "I won! I beat them easily!"

Mother hugged him and said, "That's wonderful, baby. I'm so proud of you."

The rest of us just laughed, knowing we could've beaten him if we'd been paying more attention. But watching John revel in his victory was worth it.

As the sun continued to beat down, we lay in the carriage, my brothers and I exhausted from the heat. My mother and the other women gazed out into the woods. Eventually, the thick trees began to thin out, replaced by houses in the distance.

Suddenly, my mother, still peering back, exclaimed, "I think I just saw a sign that said, 'Welcome to Charlotte!'"

Instantly, we all sat up, and I asked, "What does that mean?"

She turned to us, her eyes bright with hope. "This is where we were separated from your father! Hopefully, the carriage will stop here."

Excitement buzzed among my brothers and me as the carriage began to slow down.

One of the women leaned forward and said, "I think we're stopping."

My mother's face lit up with a wide smile, and she exclaimed, "Let's go find your father!"

My heart pounding with joy, I shouted, "We're *finally* home!"

CHAPTER 6

Home Sweet Home

As my mother hurriedly helped my brothers and me off the carriage, we waved goodbye to the other women, who stayed seated.

I thought, *I'm going to miss those ladies. They were kind.*

It seemed this wasn't their stop. I wondered how many more stops the carriage would make, considering we'd been on it since leaving the plantation, aside from our brief stop in Knoxville.

Stepping off the carriage felt like a breath of fresh air—it felt like home. I was overjoyed to be in North Carolina, the place we'd heard so much about, especially in connection to Father. My brothers and I had often dreamed of this moment, and now that it had come, it felt surreal. I knew my mother had been praying for this day as well, and I was especially happy for her.

As we walked down the road with the other former slaves, John asked, "Where are we going?" Mother responded, "I'm not sure yet. But we'll figure it out."

Elmer stated, "I hope there's food where we're headed."

Mother grinned. "I'm sure there will be," she said reassuringly.

While walking, I couldn't help but think about the beds we had slept in at the former slave quarters. I hoped we'd have something like that again tonight. The idea of going back to sleeping on the floor didn't sit well with me.

After what felt like miles of walking in the heat, we arrived at a tall building where people stood outside, guiding us in. Inside, we were led to a large room filled with tables, chairs, and boxes of food.

My brothers and I eagerly found a seat and opened our boxes. It was sandwiches and chips again, but we didn't mind. After years of eating the master's leftovers, we were grateful for any meal of our own. We ate happily.

Once we finished, my mother said we needed to find out where we'd sleep for the night.

I shouted, "I hope it's like the former slave quarters!"

John quickly agreed, "Me too!"

Mother left the room to inquire. She asked one of the people who had guided us earlier, "Is there a place for us to stay tonight?"

The woman nodded and said, "Yes, upstairs to the right, there are rooms available. Just choose any vacant one."

"Thank you!" Mother exclaimed, and we all grinned as we made our way up the stairs.

When we entered the room, I was amazed to find a gigantic bed taking up most of the space. There was even a small bathroom with a tub.

John pointed at the tub and asked Elmer, "What is that?"

Elmer chuckled, "That's where you bathe."

JOY IN SORROW, HOPE FOR TOMORROW: REUNION

John looked puzzled. Mother confirmed, "Yes, it is. Now, let's take turns washing up so we can get ready for bed."

This was the first time we'd had a room all to ourselves without other former slaves around.

On the bathroom counter sat a bar of soap and some washcloths. My brothers went in first, and then Mother and I took our turn.

Once we were all cleaned up, Mother gathered us together and said, "Let us pray." She added, "We have a long day ahead tomorrow. We need to find a more permanent place to stay."

I wanted to ask when we would see Father, but I stayed quiet, knowing that Mother already had a lot on her mind.

So, we all begin to whisper,

"Oh, Lord, Father in heaven,
We thank you for our freedom.
You have freed us from being slaves.
You have taken us away from our evil master.

We worship and adore you.
We knew that you were the only one
Who could free us.
So we didn't complain and fuss
Because we knew one day, we were going to see you.

So we kept waiting,
Until that victorious and glorious day came.
We didn't sneak away from slavery and run.
We just kept praying.

While we were believing and trusting in you,
We still had joy in sorrow.
And that gave us hope for tomorrow
Because we knew soon came our breakthrough.
Lord, we love you. Amen."

The next morning, as we woke up, John stretched and said, "I like this bed. It's comfortable."

I nodded in agreement, and Mother smiled warmly.

"Let's get ready to go," she said.

Since we didn't have any extra clothes, we stayed in what we wore the day before. As we made our way downstairs, we saw other former slaves leaving their rooms too. When we reached the bottom, people guided us back to the large room where we had eaten before. My mother, brothers, and I found a table and ate quietly.

Once we finished, Mother announced, "Let's go find somewhere to stay!"

"Yes, ma'am," we all replied.

As we stepped outside, the heat hit us immediately. The sun was blazing down, and I couldn't help but blurt out, "It's hot!"

Billy agreed, fanning himself, and Mother mentioned that we needed to find some housing information soon. She had heard that some former slaves were finding shelter with local families.

As we walked, Billy asked the question we all had on our minds: "When will we see Father?"

Mother sighed and replied, "Hopefully soon."

While we continued down the street, we passed a store on the corner with a sign in the window.

Mother squinted at it and said, "That might be a place where we can stay if I work for them."

JOY IN SORROW, HOPE FOR TOMORROW: REUNION

My brothers and I exchanged hopeful glances.

"Let me go see," Mother added, heading toward the store's back door.

We waited patiently as she disappeared inside.

When Mother returned, she told us the store clerk mentioned a woman named Mrs. Sue Lynn, who lived about eight blocks up the road.

I thought to myself, *In this heat, that's going to be a long walk.*

As we made our way toward Mrs. Sue Lynn's house, Billy suddenly asked, "Did that sign in the window say 'No Children'?"

"Yes," Mother admitted, "but I know God will make a way out of no way."

Billy fell silent, and though I didn't say it out loud, I was thinking, we probably didn't have many other options.

HELP WANTED

- **FREE Room and Board in exchange for work**

Duties Include: Cooking, Cleaning, and Caring for three children

- **If interested, Stop by:**

Mrs. Sue Lynn

113 Sherwood Ave.

(No Children Please)

Halfway there, John groaned, "I'm tired!"

Elmer asked, "Can we take a break? My feet are killing me!"

Finally, Mother found a tree with some shade for us to sit under. The heat was overwhelming, so I was relieved to rest in the cool shade.

"This feels so good," I said.

Mother smiled and reassured us, "We're almost there."

"That's great!" Billy replied enthusiastically.

We finally arrived at Mrs. Sue Lynn's house.

Mother walked up the steps and knocked on the door.

After a moment, a woman opened it and asked, "Can I help you?"

Mother smiled politely and replied, "I'm Ana Mae. I'm here about the 'Help Wanted' sign."

While eyeing us, the woman said, "I'm Sue Lynn. Are those your children?"

"Yes, ma'am," Mother responded proudly. "That's Betsy, she's sixteen. That's Billy, he's fourteen; Elmer, thirteen; and John, ten. They're wonderful children."

Mrs. Sue Lynn shared, "I have three boys of my own, ages five, seven, and ten. How do you plan on caring for my boys along with your four?"

I glanced at my mother, who remained calm and confident.

She said, "Ma'am, my children and I have traveled from Memphis, Tennessee, through Knoxville, and now we're here in Charlotte. No matter where we were, I made sure my children were fed, clothed, and had a place to sleep. I'll do the same for yours if given the chance."

JOY IN SORROW, HOPE FOR TOMORROW: REUNION

My brothers and I exchanged proud grins.

Mrs. Sue Lynn paused, then nodded. "I know my sign said 'No Children.' But if you managed to care for your four through all that, I trust you can handle my three. Come on in," she said warmly. "I'll tell Jimmy, the store clerk, to take down the sign."

We followed her inside, feeling hopeful for the first time in a while.

CHAPTER 7

Room and Board

When we stepped into the house, three boys came running toward us.

Happily, Mrs. Sue Lynn introduced them, "This is Joshua, he's ten. Timothy is seven, and Adam, he's five."

"Hello," we all said in unison.

Joshua quickly added, "You can call me Josh."

Timothy chimed in, "They call me Timmy."

After introductions, Mrs. Sue Lynn led us to the room where we'd be staying. It was spacious with a huge bed big enough for all of us.

My mother looked around and said, "This is perfect. Thank you."

Mrs. Sue Lynn smiled and said, "I'll let you all settle in while I start on dinner." Elmer grinned, and she continued, "The bathroom is down the hall to your left."

"Thank you!" we all echoed.

She gently reminded her sons to give us some privacy, and as they left, it felt like a rare luxury to have the space to ourselves.

As Mrs. Sue Lynn and her boys walked away, Billy asked, "How big is this house?"

Mother replied, "From the looks of it, pretty big. Now, let's get cleaned up for dinner."

John, naturally, was the first to dart into the bathroom. He didn't even complain about needing to use it, which surprised me. Meanwhile, Billy, Elmer, and I stretched out on the bed. It was soft, a nice change after the long, sun-filled walk.

Suddenly, Mother said, "Stay here. I'm going to help Mrs. Sue Lynn in the kitchen."

"Yes, ma'am," we replied.

Not long after, Josh, Timmy, and Adam came back into the room. Josh invited us to their room, saying they had toys to play with. When John came from the bathroom, he immediately introduced himself, and the rest of us did the same.

Timmy asked John, "You want to come play in our room?"

John glanced at me, and I informed him, "We can't. Mother said to stay here."

John sighed in disappointment and mumbled, "Okay."

Billy, always practical, suggested, "Well, they can play here!"

So we stayed, sitting on the bed and chatting. We shared stories about ourselves, and they told us about their school and their friends.

I thought to myself, *Maybe one day we'll go to school and make friends too.*

Eventually, Mother returned and called us to the kitchen for dinner.

As we followed her, she introduced herself to the boys, "I'm Ana Mae, and I'll be cooking, cleaning, and taking care of you."

They nodded without a word.

JOY IN SORROW, HOPE FOR TOMORROW: REUNION

When we entered the kitchen, Mrs. Sue Lynn was already seated at the table. She welcomed us to sit down as Mother served the food. It was a simple meal, but the warmth of it made it feel like a feast. After so long without a hot meal, we were all grateful.

After dinner, Mother asked us to wait in the room while she stayed to wash the dishes. Josh, Timmy, and Adam said good night and headed to their room. My brothers and I lay on the bed, talking about how nice the boys were and how much we liked them.

I listened to the faint sounds of conversation between Mrs. Sue Lynn and my mother from the kitchen.

Mrs. Sue Lynn mentioned that she was a widow, and I wondered, *What does that mean?*

She explained that her husband, Adam—after whom little Adam was named—had died from a terminal illness. Hearing this made me feel sad for her. I couldn't imagine losing someone like that.

When Mother finally returned, she told us to get ready for bed. I asked, "What's a widow?"

Mother looked at me curiously and asked, "Why do you ask?"

"I heard Mrs. Sue Lynn say she was a widow," I explained.

Mother nodded and said, "A widow is a woman whose husband has died and she hasn't remarried. Now, let's pray."

We all knelt together at the foot of the bed.

Then we all begin to whisper,

> *"Oh, Lord, Father in heaven,*
> *We thank you for our freedom.*
> *You have freed us from being slaves.*
> *You have taken us away from our evil master.*

VONNETTA MAYO

We worship and adore you.
We knew that you were the only one
Who could free us.
So we didn't complain and fuss
Because we knew one day, we were going to see you.

So we kept waiting,
Until that victorious and glorious day came.
We didn't sneak away from slavery and run.
We just kept praying.

While we were believing and trusting in you,
We still had joy in sorrow.
And that gave us hope for tomorrow
Because we knew soon came our breakthrough.
Lord, we love you. Amen."

My brothers and I crawled into the huge bed, and Mother instructed the boys to sleep at the foot while she and I took the head. My brothers grinned, clearly liking the arrangement of not having to sleep next to my mother and me. Once everyone was settled, Mother quietly closed the door and joined us in the bed.

CHAPTER 8

School in Session

When my brothers and I woke up the next morning, we noticed Mother was already up.

John immediately said, "I want to play with Timmy and Josh in their room."

I replied, "I don't know where Mother is. Maybe she'll be back soon."

So we waited anxiously for her return. When she walked into the room, she told us there were washcloths in the bathroom and that we should take turns bathing.

She handed us some clothes from Mrs. Sue Lynn, explaining, "These are from her sons' closet." She then added, "After your bath, come to the kitchen to eat."

I quickly volunteered, "I'll go first."

The bathtub in this house was much bigger than the one we had used before, and soaking in the hot water felt amazing. After my turn, my brothers bathed while I went to the kitchen.

Mother had prepared eggs and ham, which tasted delicious.

I asked, "Where are Mrs. Sue Lynn and the boys?"

"The boys went to school, and Mrs. Sue Lynn has errands to run," Mother replied.

Shortly after, my brothers joined us in the kitchen, and Billy asked, "Are Josh, Timmy, and Adam here?"

I exhaled and said, "No, they're at school."

John pouted and admitted, "I wanted to play with them."

Mother comforted him by saying, "Maybe after school, you'll get the chance." She then started washing the dishes while we headed back to our room.

As we lay on the bed, Elmer suggested, "I'm going to ask Mother if we can go outside."

I thought it was a great idea. We hadn't been outside much since arriving.

"It would be nice to get some fresh air," I added, and John and Billy grinned in agreement.

When Mother came in, Elmer asked, "Can we go outside?"

She nodded, "We can sit on the porch for a bit."

Once outside, the heat was intense, but we were happy just to be together, teasing each other on the porch steps. Mother sat in a chair, watching us as people passed by, some waving and others staring as if we didn't belong. We didn't let it bother us, continuing to joke around and enjoy each other's company.

After some time in the sun, Mother called, "Let's go back inside. Mrs. Sue Lynn and the boys will be home soon."

We quickly headed indoors, and while Mother went to the kitchen, we headed to our room.

As I sat on the bed, I wondered, *Is she cooking again?*

She was always in the kitchen, but I knew better than to offer help—she would never let me.

We eventually dozed off, but we were awakened by Mrs. Sue Lynn shouting, "Go do your homework!"

We heard Josh, Timmy, and Adam running around the house.

John immediately asked, "Can we go play with them?"

I replied, "It sounds like they're about to do their homework now."

John frowned and said, "Okay."

While I listened to the conversation in the kitchen, I could hear Mother asking Mrs. Sue Lynn to taste some meat she had cooked.

Mrs. Sue Lynn responded with, "That's good." Then she called out, "Boys, hurry up with your homework! Dinner's almost ready!"

Billy suggested, "Let's go check if they're done."

"Let's go!" I agreed, and we all headed to their room.

I was surprised by how enormous their room was, easily twice the size of ours, with each boy having his own bed.

John asked, "Can we play with your toys now?"

Josh shook his head, then explained, "We have to finish our homework first."

"What kind of homework is it?" I asked.

"Math," Josh replied.

"Can you teach us?" I asked.

Josh smiled and agreed, showing us how to add and subtract. It was fun learning from him and Timmy, though John sometimes got frustrated when he couldn't grasp the concepts right away.

I encouraged him by saying, "The more we practice, the better we'll get."

Even though they were younger, the boys were teaching us. They knew we hadn't been to school. Back on the plantation, Mother had taught us what little she could in between her long hours of working in the fields. Although Josh and John were the same age, we didn't know who was older because we didn't know John's birthday.

Finally, after we worked through several math problems, the boys finished their homework. Adam was just about to pull out their toys when Mother appeared at the door.

"Dinner's ready," she announced.

We all went to the kitchen, sat around the table with Mrs. Sue Lynn, and Mother served us our meal. After we finished eating, I complimented Mother, telling her the food was delicious. Now I understood why Mrs. Sue Lynn had said the meat was good.

John, still hopeful, asked, "Can we go back to the boys' room to play?"

But Mrs. Sue Lynn gently said, "Sorry, but the boys need to get ready for bed. They have school tomorrow."

John lowered his head in disappointment, and we made our way back to our room.

"I'll be in shortly," Mother called after us.

"Yes, ma'am," we responded.

Back in our room, John grumbled, "We're never going to get a chance to play with their toys."

The rest of us stayed silent. A little while later, Mother came in.

"Time to lie down," she stated.

After she closed the door, we all knelt at the foot of the bed to pray.

We all begin to whisper,

JOY IN SORROW, HOPE FOR TOMORROW: REUNION

"Oh, Lord, Father in heaven,
We thank you for our freedom.
You have freed us from being slaves.
You have taken us away from our evil master.

We worship and adore you.
We knew that you were the only one
Who could free us.
So we didn't complain and fuss
Because we knew one day, we were going to see you.

So we kept waiting,
Until that victorious and glorious day came.
We didn't sneak away from slavery and run.
We just kept praying.

While we were believing and trusting in you,
We still had joy in sorrow.
And that gave us hope for tomorrow
Because we knew soon came our breakthrough.
Lord, we love you. Amen."

Even though it hadn't been long since my brothers and I woke up from our nap, I still felt a bit tired. As I lay back, reflecting on the day and the math problems we solved, I could feel my eyes growing heavy. Just before drifting into a deep sleep, I imagined the moment when my mother, brothers, and I would finally reunite with my father. The thought brought a smile to my face.

CHAPTER 9

Peace

The next morning, when we woke up, my mother was already out of bed.

I figured she must be in the kitchen, so I said to my brothers, "Let's go eat."

When we arrived, she was standing over the stove. Without turning around, she said, "Breakfast is almost ready."

John grinned. Shortly after, Mother served us our hot meal.

As we ate, I asked, "Is Mrs. Sue Lynn running errands again today?"

"I'm not sure," Mother replied. "When she left, she just said she'd be back."

After breakfast, Mother told us to get cleaned up.

"Can we go outside?" Elmer asked.

"Yes, once I'm done cleaning," she responded. She added, "Your clothes are in the bathroom."

"Yes, ma'am," we said in unison as we headed to our room.

When we got there, I quickly claimed, "I'll go first."

I liked going first because it meant I didn't have to wait for my brothers to finish splashing around in the tub. Once we were all done, we sat in the room waiting for Mother. Elmer was eager to go outside, and John agreed. I just hoped it wasn't too hot.

As time passed, we began playing and wrestling around. I was sure all the noise would make Mother shout, "Stop making all that noise!"

But she didn't, so we kept on wrestling until she finally came in and announced, "It's time to go outside."

This time she said we could play in the yard instead of just the porch. She did remind us there were areas we weren't allowed to go, so most of our outdoor time would still be spent on the porch or in the front yard. That didn't bother us; we were happy enough playing wherever we could.

Not long after we got outside, Mrs. Sue Lynn and her boys came through the gate.

John yelled, "Hey, Josh, Timmy, and Adam!"

"Hello," they replied.

Timmy asked, "Can we play outside?"

"Yes, but first, put your schoolwork indoors," Mrs. Sue Lynn said.

John smiled. My mother stayed outdoors as Mrs. Sue Lynn went inside. When the boys quickly returned, they joined in a game of "Tag" with us. We had so much fun I didn't even notice the heat.

After several rounds, Mother called out, "It's time to come inside now. The boys have to do their homework, and I need to start dinner."

Back in the house, Mother went to the kitchen, the boys to their room, and my brothers and I to ours, collapsing on the bed from exhaustion. As we lay there, I overheard Mother and Mrs. Sue Lynn talking and laughing in the kitchen. I'd *never* heard my mother laugh like that before. It was infectious, and before long, both women were giggling uncontrollably. Hearing it made me chuckle.

Billy asked, "Did you hear that?"

"Yes. Mother's laughing," I replied.

My brothers smiled.

"I'm happy for her," Elmer said. "Let's go see if the boys are done with their homework," he suggested.

"Sure," I said. "Maybe they can teach us what they learned today."

When we got to their room, Josh and Timmy were finishing their reading.

"Can you teach us how to read?" I asked.

"Of course!" Josh said.

He began reading aloud while we followed along. Afterward, I gave it a try, and Josh helped me with some words I couldn't pronounce. I was grateful for his patience, as this became our daily routine: after school, the boys would teach us what they'd learned.

Meanwhile, John and Adam grew bored and started playing with Adam's toys. Thereafter, Timmy joined in, and Billy and Elmer followed him. Josh eventually joined them, but I stayed focused on reading, enjoying the new words I was learning. It wasn't long before Mother came in, signaling it was time for dinner. We headed to the kitchen, and as always, the meal was delicious.

After dinner, Mother told us to get ready for bed. We quickly obeyed, still worn out from the day.

As we walked to our room, John shouted, "Good night, Josh, Timmy, and Adam!"

"Good night!" they echoed.

The moment we got to our room, we climbed into bed.

"I had fun playing with their toys," John said. "I can't wait to play again tomorrow."

Elmer agreed. I looked over at Billy, who was already half asleep. I hoped Mother would come in soon so we could say "Our Nightly Prayer" before I drifted off.

"How long do you think Mother's going to be in the kitchen?" Elmer asked.

"Hopefully not long," I replied. "I'm ready to pray and go to sleep."

"Me too," Billy mumbled sleepily.

Finally, Mother came in and exclaimed, "Let us pray!"

My brothers and I climbed out of bed.

And louder than usual, we begin to pray,

"Oh, Lord, Father in heaven,
We thank you for our freedom.
You have freed us from being slaves.
You have taken us away from our evil master.

We worship and adore you.
We knew that you were the only one
Who could free us.
So we didn't complain and fuss
Because we knew one day, we were going to see you.

JOY IN SORROW, HOPE FOR TOMORROW: REUNION

So we kept waiting,
Until that victorious and glorious day came.
We didn't sneak away from slavery and run.
We just kept praying.

While we were believing and trusting in you,
We still had joy in sorrow.
And that gave us hope for tomorrow
Because we knew soon came our breakthrough.
Lord, we love you. Amen."

As I lay there, it dawned on me that Mother hadn't mentioned Father in a while. I knew he must still be on her mind, and I hoped she hadn't given up on seeing him.

I wondered, *We couldn't have come all this way not to see him, right?*

CHAPTER 10

Deliverance

When we finally woke up the next day, it was well into the morning.

Not long after we stirred, Mother came into the room and said, "Finally, you're all awake. Breakfast was done hours ago."

"Can we still eat?" Elmer asked eagerly.

"Of course. You can have some cereal," Mother replied, which made Elmer grin.

"Cereal!" John exclaimed in confusion.

"Yes, cornflakes with cold milk," Mother confirmed.

We rushed to the kitchen, sat down at the table, and watched as Mother poured us bowls of cereal and milk. John enjoyed it so much that he asked for another serving, which Mother gladly gave him.

After we finished eating, she said, "Now, go get dressed. Mrs. Sue Lynn left me a note to pick up a few things from the corner store."

"Yes, ma'am," we replied in unison.

Curious, Billy asked, "Is it the same corner store that had the sign in the window?"

"Yes, it is," Mother answered, and we headed to our room to change.

Once inside, Elmer groaned, "That's a long walk to the store!"

"I know," I agreed, hoping it wouldn't be too hot outside as I made my way to the bathroom.

While we got dressed, Mother tidied up the kitchen. Secretly, I hoped she might change her mind about going. The thought of that long walk didn't sound appealing.

But soon enough, Mother came into the room and insisted that we head out to the store before Mrs. Sue Lynn and the boys returned.

As we exited the front door, she reassured us, "This walk will not be bad."

I was glad to hear that and even more relieved when we stepped outside to cool pleasant weather. The breeze rustled the trees, creating a peaceful atmosphere.

As we walked, my brothers and I played around, teasing and wrestling each other.

John, however, eventually got fed up and stopped playing, which made Mother laugh.

"Stop bothering my baby!" she joked, hugging John as we all laughed together.

It felt so good to laugh with her, something we had never done like that before. Even though we had been free for a while, I had never felt the kind of freedom I did walking to the corner store with my mother and brothers. We were so wrapped up in enjoying ourselves that the distance didn't seem to matter. Before we realized it, we were already there.

When we arrived, we followed Mother to the store's rear entrance. She handed the store clerk, Jimmy, the note from Mrs. Sue Lynn. After reading it, Jimmy waved us inside.

Instantly, as we stepped in, John asked, "Are there any toys here?"

Jimmy answered, "Not many."

Mother added, "Let's get what we need."

She took her time walking through the aisles, carefully selecting the items. Although the store wasn't enormous, I didn't expect to see it all in one day. But my mother did. She wasn't in any rush, which surprised me. Eventually, she gathered all the items and headed to the counter.

As we waited by the back door, I saw Mother take some cash from her pocket and hand it to Jimmy. It must have been money from Mrs. Sue Lynn because I hadn't seen Mother with any since we came to the plantation. Once the transaction was complete, we began to leave the store.

Just as we were stepping out, a man approached the rear entrance.

Suddenly, Mother gasped, "That's Billy Sr.!"

I quickly glanced at her, then back at the man.

Billy, wide-eyed, asked, "Is that Father?"

"Yes, children, that's your father," Mother confirmed.

We stood there, speechless, staring at him. As he smiled at us, I realized he was even more than I had *ever* imagined.

VONNETTA MAYO

The End

About the Author

Vonnetta Mayo was born in Gary, Indiana, and raised in Southern California. She then relocated to the Sunshine State, Florida. Afterward she lived in Morgantown, West Virginia, for a couple of years. Then she moved to New Bremen, Ohio. Now she resides back in the Sunshine State, Florida.

Vonnetta Mayo is the youngest of four children. At an early age, she aspired to become a writer. Vonnetta Mayo's mother and father both were influential in her becoming a writer. She started writing poems for church conventions. As a teenager, Vonnetta Mayo won an essay contest and received a college scholarship. At the University of California, San Diego, she minored in literature and writing. That is where her goal of becoming a writer emerged.

Vonnetta Mayo loves God and attributes her inspiration for writing to God. She was raised in the church. That is where she acquired most of her teachings and beliefs. She believes in pursuing and never giving up on your dreams. Therefore, Vonnetta Mayo is the proud author of a two-book series, *Joy in Sorrow, Hope for Tomorrow* and *Joy in Sorrow, Hope for Tomorrow: Homecoming*, and a memoir, *Charlene Marshall: My Extraordinary Odyssey*. Readers' Favorite Five-Stars Review Recipient and Literary Titan Gold Book Award Winner Vonnetta Mayo thanks God for making her dream of becoming an author come true.

www.ingramcontent.com/pod-product-compliance
Lightning Source LLC
Chambersburg PA
CBHW050452250125
20773CB00015B/210